Thar She Blows!

For Laura, my little adventurer — S.K.

*To my granddaughter, Jessica
and supportive husband, Al* — P.F.

Copyright © 1997 Trudy Corporation, 353 Main Avenue, Norwalk, CT 06851,
and the Smithsonian Institution, Washington, DC, 20560.

Soundprints is a division of Trudy Corporation, Norwalk, Connecticut.

Book Design: Shields & Partners, Westport, CT

First Edition 1997
10 9 8 7 6 5 4 3 2 1
Printed in Hong Kong

Library of Congress Cataloging-in-Publication Data

Kassirer, Sue.

Thar she blows : whaling in the 1860s /
by Sue Kassirer : illustrated by Pat Fridell.
      p.   cm.
Summary: While visiting a whaling exhibit at the Museum of Natural History, Emma suddenly finds herself transported back in time to a nineteenth century whaling ship.
     ISBN 1-56899-507-5 (hardcover)   ISBN 1-56899-508-3 (pbk.)
1. Whaling — Fiction. [1. Time travel — Fiction.] I. Fridell, Pat, 1930- ill. II. Title.
     P27.K1562Th 1997   97-10793
     [E] — dc21   CIP
                                             AC

Thar She Blows!

Written by Sue Kassirer
Illustrated by Pat Fridell

Soundprints
Where Children Discover…

"Look at the size of that whale!" says Emma, pointing to the vast panorama in front of her. "It's nearly as big as the ship."

Emma and her friends Lucy, Kevin, and Tomas are visiting the Whaling Exhibit at the Smithsonian Institution's National Museum of American History. It's a cold and rainy day, and the four friends are happy to be inside.

As Emma reads about the exhibit, she straightens her shoulders and lifts her head high. "My great-great-great grandfather, Randall Washington, was a harpooner on a whaling ship back in the 1840s."

"Really?" says Tomas.

"He actually threw the harpoon into the whale?" says Lucy. "Yes," Emma answered. "People back then hunted whales to make lamp oil and other things out of whale blubber. This was before there was electricity."

"Listen to this," says Kevin. "They also used something called spermaceti. They got it out of the whale's skull and used it to make candles, detergents, and machine oil."

While Lucy, Tomas, and Kevin read more about whaling, Emma thinks about Randall Washington and the wonderful stories she has heard about him since she was small. She remembers one story in particular.

"There's a beautiful ivory ring that's been in my mother's china cabinet for as long as I can remember," Emma tells her friends. "Randall Washington made it while he was away on a whaling voyage."

"He made a ring while he was hunting whales?" asks Kevin in disbelief. "Why'd he do that?"

"A lot of time on whaling ships was spent waiting to spot whales. The sailors needed something to do when they weren't working, so they carved beautiful things out of whale teeth and whalebones — often for their wives or girlfriends. They called it scrimshawing.

"Randall planned on proposing marriage to my great-great-great grandmother Elisa with this ring. He finished it the week before they were to come into port."

"But that night there was a terrible storm at sea, and Randall lost the ring. Somehow he got it back and was able to propose. Everyone's always wondered exactly what happened."

As Emma tells the story, her gaze moves to the whaling panorama mounted on the wall behind the boat. The deep blue water seems to shimmer.

Cold water splashes against Emma's face.

Where is that water coming from? she thinks. *We're in the exhibit, but —oh, my gosh!*

Emma looks around quickly and sees that she's standing on the deck of a large ship that's rolling with the waves. It looks just like one of the model whalers in the exhibit. There's a cold autumn wind, and everyone on deck is being sprayed with salt water.

Emma looks down and sees that she is holding a harpoon in her hands.

Chained to the ship's side is an enormous whale that is being cut into long strips. Its body is turned around and around as it's being cut. With each turn, the ship lurches with the weight of the mammoth beast.

"That was a whopper of a sperm whale you got there, Randall!" a man yells to Emma as he hoists a large piece of blubber aboard. "It surely was!" several other men add.

"But I'm not Randall — " Emma's words are drowned out by the sound of the whale's carcass as it bumps the side of the ship.

It can't be, Emma tells herself. *Somehow, I've gone back to the 1840s, and everybody thinks I'm Randall Washington. I think I just harpooned this whale!*

Before Emma has a chance to think over what is happening to her, there is a call for dinner.

"Grub, ho!" a steward shouts.

"Time for the usual — beans, rice, and salt junk," says one of the men, who is also carrying a harpoon. *He doesn't sound very excited,* thinks Emma, but she follows him anyway.

"Hallo, Jason, hallo, Randall," says a man who is already seated at the table.

"Lobscouse!" both men exclaim in delight as piping hot food is placed upon the table.

"It sometimes pays to be a harpooner. You can bet the crew won't be gettin' this special fare," says Jason as he and his mate devour the food set before them.

Emma takes a small bite of the unfamiliar food the men have called lobscouse and finds it is easy to clean her plate. The food reminds her of the tasty corned beef hash her mother makes, only it's much saltier.

"Well, I guess it is time to start waiting again," says Jason. "Could be days before we'll spot another big one."

Emma is relieved to hear Jason's words. She's not sure how she feels about killing whales. But, she also is surprised to find that she is looking forward to the challenge and excitement of hunting a whale.

"Come along!" says Jason. Emma follows as Jason makes his way up on deck, where many of the crew are smoking pipes, reading, and singing songs.

Several men are holding small items and carving them. One man is making a long object that looks like a rolling pin, another some clothespins, and still another a set of chess pieces. Emma feels her heart quicken as she realizes they're scrimshawing.

"Hallo, Randall my friend. Do you still plan on asking the young lady for her hand?" asks a dark-haired sailor. "Not long now before we dock in New Bedford. And how, may I ask, is that ring coming along?"

"Very well, indeed," Emma says. She feels in her pocket. Sure enough, a small round object is there. And next to it, Emma feels a pocket knife. Emma takes them both out.

This ring looks just like the one in the china cabinet at home, Emma thinks with excitement. *Just a small area still needs to be carved.*

Emma watches the men and sees that scrimshawing is not much different from the whittling she has enjoyed doing at home with her grandfather. She eagerly sets to work.

"Randall, it's been a long day," says Jason after a while. "Shall we get some rest?"

Emma looks up with a start. She has become so absorbed in her scrimshawing that she has lost track of time. With a yawn, she follows Jason to their bunks.

But just as Emma is about to climb into her bunk bed, she realizes what she has done. Having taken so naturally to scrimshawing, she finished the ring.

That means that tonight there will be a storm at sea and I will lose the ring. Maybe I'll solve the mystery of how Randall finally found it! she tells herself.

Emma decides to hang the ring around her neck with a piece of twine. *Maybe it will stay put this way,* she thinks as the gentle rocking of the ship lulls her to sleep.

Emma is suddenly awake and finds herself being thrown to the floor beside her bunk.

"Hold on!" yells one of her bunkmates. "It's a storm, the likes of which I've not seen in years!"

Emma watches in horror as objects in the cabin crash to the deck. *A storm at sea,* she thinks. *It's happening!* She reaches for the ring and is relieved to find that it still hangs safely around her neck.

After some time, the sea becomes calm once again. Emma and her bunkmates return to their bunks. With her hand wrapped around the ring, Emma quickly falls into a deep sleep.

She is awakened by a bellowing voice. "She blows! Thar she blows!" the voice booms.

Emma's bunkmates leap up and grab their harpoons. Emma knows this means that a whale has been sighted. She breathlessly grabs her own harpoon and races on deck with the others.

The rising sun, just peeking over the horizon, casts a glorious orange light over the ocean. And sure enough, not far in the distance, Emma spots a huge creature emerging from the still water.

"It's another sperm whale, and a mighty one at that!" yells one of the men.

"Lower away!" someone calls out, and three boats are lowered into the water.

Emma quickly climbs down the side of the ship and leaps into one of the boats. Then, looking for Jason, she sees that he and another harpooner are each holding an oar and sitting in the bows of the other two boats. Quickly, she takes her place in the third.

"Throw in the harpoon line!" one of the men shouts, and a tub of rope is lowered into the boat. Emma ties the rope to the blunt end of her harpoon.

To Emma's surprise, the three boats begin racing one another. Each wants to get to the whale first!

Before she knows it, Emma's boat is within yards of the whale. The huge animal heaves its great body up and down, in and out of the water, with a force that seems to say, "I am much bigger than you, and this is my ocean!"

"Harpooner, stand by your iron!" the man at the helm calls out.

With the whale so near, and everything happening so fast, Emma reacts without thinking. She stands up and raises her harpoon. Then she takes a deep breath and, with all her strength, plunges the barbed head into the whale's body.

The mammoth creature jerks for a moment and then starts swimming away, pulling the harpoon line — and the boat — with it.

"Why, it's a Nantucket Sleigh Ride," one of the men calls. "Hold on for dear life — and get ready for a drenching!"

Emma grabs the sides of the boat as the whale yanks it rapidly over the waves. *It's just like waterskiing,* Emma tells herself, *only we're being pulled by a sperm whale, and who knows when he'll stop!*

Slowly but surely, the whale seems to weaken and begins to slow down.

"Headsman, take over!" one of the men commands.

With that, the mate raises a lance high in the air, and sticks it deep into the mammal's body. The whale swims around and around, in smaller and smaller circles, and finally lies still.

"We've got it," someone yells out.

With the excitement of the chase over, Emma realizes that she has forgotten about the scrimshaw ring. She reaches for the twine around her neck and finds that it's gone — and so is the ring! Emma's heart beats fast. Could the ring have fallen overboard?

Emma quickly searches the bottom of the boat, but all she sees is re-coiled harpoon line. *How will I ever find it now?* she thinks.

Slowly the men row the boat and its heavy cargo back to the ship.

Emma is proud that she harpooned the whale, but now her mind is on one thing only — the ring. She must find it.

Safely back at the ship, the sailors climb up onto the deck. "You did it again, Randall!" one of them calls out and gives Emma a friendly clap on the shoulder. "You're a natural born harpooner if ever I saw one!"

As Emma steps onto the deck, she feels something hard in her boot. "Ouch!" she calls out.

"Whale bit ya?" says one of the crew with a laugh.

"I think so!" Emma pulls off her boot and shakes it out.

A small object falls to the deck. It's a scrimshaw ring — *the* scrimshaw ring! Emma grabs it and clasps it tightly. *I found it,* she thinks happily. *Just like I was supposed to.*

With a happy sigh, Emma stares at the ocean. The water starts to shimmer, and Emma is momentarily blinded. When she can focus again, she is staring at the American Whaling Exhibit at the Smithsonian, twisting the small birthstone ring on her finger.

"Come on, Emma!" yells Lucy. "Did you know your hair is still wet from the rain?"

"Really?" says Emma. She touches her hair, and just as she does, a drop of water slides down her face. Out of curiosity she opens her mouth for a split second and catches the drop on the tip of her tongue.

Salt water — I knew it! Emma thinks. She smiles as she follows Lucy to the next exhibit.

A Short History of American Whaling

People have hunted whales for food, fuel, and as material for tools since prehistoric times. In North America, Inuit and Native Americans hunted whales as far back as 100 A.D.

In the 1600s, the English colonists began whaling along the shores of the Massachusetts Bay Colony. Whales called "right whales" supplied the colonists with oil for lamps and candles. The first American whaling companies were formed in Easthampton and Southampton, on Long Island, New York, as well as on Nantucket, an island off the coast of Massachusetts.

It wasn't until the early eighteenth century — with the discovery of the sperm whale, found only in deep waters — that whalers began to venture out into the ocean. Dutch, English, and American whaling ships began sailing the seas.

In the early days of whaling, a North American crew was a mixed group of Yankees, Native Americans, and some African Americans. As the industry boomed, and more men were needed, half the crew often came from other countries.

A whaling voyage could last as long as four years and could take the crew around the world. Life on board was anything but easy. Quarters were cramped, stuffy, and often infested with insects. The pay was low, and crew members were charged for clothing and other necessities during the course of the voyage. Many a whaleman ended a voyage in debt to his ship!

Why did men go whaling? They went for adventure, for a job, and for the possibility of advancement from forecastle hand (an ordinary member of the crew) to harpooner or tradesman, to officer (third, second, and first mate), and maybe, with hard work and luck, to captain.

By the mid-nineteenth century, the United States led the world whaling industry, with more than 700 ships sailing the seas. But all of this changed abruptly with the discovery of petroleum, in Pennsylvania, in 1859.

An era had ended. Whale oil, which had once been so valuable that it was used as currency, was no longer needed to light the lamps of the world. But, because of whaling America had changed. American men traveled farther from home than they ever dreamed they would. Some families made their fortune. Beautiful pieces of scrimshaw, many still in existence, found their places in American homes. And, last but not least, a love for adventure was forever planted in the American imagination.

Glossary

blubber: the fatty part of a whale that is cut out and "tried out," or boiled down, to oil

bow: the front of a boat or ship

harpoon: an iron shaft with a barbed head attached to a long wooden handle and used to spear a whale

headsman: the captain or mate who steers the boat. Once the harpooner spears the whale, the headsman trades places with him and kills the whale with a lance

helm: the wheel or tiller by which a ship is steered

lance: a pointed, metal-headed spear used for killing a harpooned whale

lobscouse: a hash of salt meat and hard bread, cooked as a treat once or twice a week on a whaler

Nantucket Sleigh Ride: the fast ride across the waves that the harpooned whale, attached by the harpoon line, sometimes gave the men and their boat

scrimshawing: the art of carving and decorating whale teeth and pieces of jawbone. Practically every whaleman produced pieces of scrimshaw for his wife, girlfriend, mother, or others back home. This time-consuming craft filled many long hours between whale sightings

sperm whale: a large and ferocious whale, which swam in deep waters and was difficult to catch. The oil it yielded was far superior to that of any other type of whale

spermaceti: fatty matter, located in the lower half of the sperm whale's forehead. It was used for making ointments and fine candles